Queen of the Pool

Story by Jan Weeks
Illustrations by Meredith Thomas

PM Chapter Books
part of the Rigby PM Collection

U.S. edition © 2001 Rigby
a division of Reed Elsevier Inc.
500 Coventry Lane
Crystal Lake, IL 60014
www.rigby.com

Text © Nelson Thomson Learning 2000
Illustrations © Nelson Thomson Learning 2000
Originally published in Australia by Nelson Thomson Learning

06 05 04 03 02 01
10 9 8 7 6 5 4 3 2 1

Queen of the Pool
ISBN 0 7635 7445 7

Printed in China by Midas Printing (Asia) Ltd.

Contents

Chapter 1

The Promotion

"Why can't we stay here?" Selena asked her father. "I like living in the country. I don't want to leave my friends."

Selena already knew the answer. Her father was a policeman. He'd been transferred to the city, and he had to start his new job in two weeks. It was a big promotion and everyone was pleased about it. Everyone except Selena, that is.

Their new house had a pool in the backyard. "Think how good that will be," her older brother Danny kept saying. "Now Mom will be able to teach us to swim."

They had never learned to swim because their town didn't have a public swimming pool.

That hadn't bothered Selena. She'd never wanted to learn to swim. Even thinking about it frightened her. When Selena was three, her family had gone to the beach for vacation.

On the first morning, Selena and Danny had had a great time running in and out of the shallow waves. That was until a big wave had knocked Selena over, bouncing her around on the sand and filling her nose and mouth with salty water.

Her father had come running, but by then a woman had pulled her out of the water. After that, Selena had refused to go anywhere near the water.

"She'll get over it," her father had said. But Selena had never forgotten how scared she'd been.

Chapter 2

Selena Settles In

Once Selena had moved to the new house in the city, she had to admit she liked it. Her bedroom was big and there was plenty of room for all her things. She could see the pool from her bedroom window.

And she liked her new school. Her teacher, Miss Gileno, made jokes all the time, and everyone laughed a lot.

Lots of children at school wanted to play with Selena at break and lunchtime. Ellie Kono was one of them. She lived across the street from Selena, and they soon became best friends.

Ellie had a baby sister named Jade who was learning to walk. Selena loved playing with her. "I wish I had a little sister," she said.

One day, Miss Gileno told the class about the swim meet that would be held in two weeks time. There were going to be races for all ages.

When Ellie asked Selena if she was going to enter, Selena shook her head. "I can't swim," she said.

"Do you think your parents would mind if I practice in your pool?" Ellie asked. She didn't have a pool in her backyard.

Selena's parents didn't mind at all. In fact, they hoped it might encourage Selena. They thought Selena should learn to swim, but they didn't want to force her.

"Just remember to keep the pool gate closed," they said. They didn't want any small children to wander in off the street and drown in their pool.

It hadn't taken Danny long to learn to swim. Before the end of the first week in their new home, he had made it across the pool.

"Come in," Danny and Ellie now begged Selena. "The water's great. You'll enjoy it."

But all Selena did was shake her head. She was happy to sit in a deckchair and watch them.

Chapter 3

The Hero

One afternoon when Selena came home from school, she found her mother sitting on the back lawn with Jade, who was playing with some toys. Selena's mother had offered to babysit Jade while Mrs. Kono went shopping with Ellie.

As usual, Danny had raced home to be first in the pool. He could now swim the length of the pool and wanted his mother to watch him.

"I'll look after Jade," said Selena. She felt tired because she had been learning to line dance at school, so she stretched out on the grass beside Jade.

While Danny was swimming, the telephone rang and their mother went inside to answer it.

Danny climbed out of the pool, flicking water onto Selena's face as he went inside to get something to eat.

Selena closed her eyes. As she drifted off to sleep, she could hear Jade talking to herself while she played with her blocks.

The next thing Selena heard was a splash. She sat up with a start and quickly looked around. She saw that Jade was no longer beside her, and that the pool gate was wide open.

Quick as a flash, Selena ran into the pool area, yelling for help as she ran.

She could see Jade in the pool, sinking to the bottom. Without even thinking of her own fear, Selena jumped in to rescue Jade. Water filled her nose and mouth, but she didn't let that stop her.

She grabbed Jade and lifted her straight up out of the water. Jade was screaming and sputtering.

Already Danny and Selena's mother were by the pool.

"Thank goodness you got to her in time," Selena's mother said, relieved that Jade was all right. She took Jade from Selena and cradled the little girl in her arms.

"I thought I shut the gate," Danny said, looking really sorry.

"And I didn't mean to fall asleep," Selena added.

"It just shows how easily accidents can happen," their mother said. "But the good thing is that Jade is all right. You're a hero, Selena. If it hadn't been for you, I hate to think what might have happened."

But all Selena could think about was what would have happened if Jade had fallen into the deep end of the pool. They might both have drowned.

Chapter 4

Safety Measures

The next afternoon, Selena was the first one home from school. Her mother was going to teach her to swim, and Selena was ready to start.

Selena noticed a new lock on the pool gate. It was self-locking. There was also a sign explaining how to give first-aid to accident victims. In the corner was a big life preserver tied to a long piece of rope.

"We should have thought about getting those things before we moved into the new house," Selena's mother said. She was already in the water, standing in the shallow end, waiting for Selena to get in.

"The first thing I want you to do is learn how to put your face in the water," her mother said. "Then I'll teach you how to kick your legs."

Chapter 5

Selena Learns to Swim

By the end of the week, Selena was using a kickboard. She even tried going into the deep end of the pool. The week after that, she didn't need a board. She could swim from one side of the pool to the other.

"It's not as hard as I thought it was going to be," Selena said.

"It's too bad you didn't learn to swim sooner," said Ellie, after she'd watched Selena swim a lap. "Then you could have raced in the swim meet we had last month."

"Well, there's always next year," Selena said, as she climbed out of the pool.

"And after that, there's always the Olympics," joked Danny, and everyone laughed.

Selena knew her brother was making fun of her, but she didn't care. She felt so pleased that she wasn't afraid of the water anymore, now that she had finally learned to swim.